THE DARK KNIGHT™

SUPER DC HEROES

THE

DARK KNIGHT

SCARECROW'S FLOCK OF FEAR

WRITTEN BY
MATTHEW K. MANNING

ILLUSTRATED BY
LUCIANO VECCHIO

BATMAN CREATED BY BOB KANE

STONE ARCH BOOKS
a capstone imprint

PUBLISHED BY STONE ARCH BOOKS IN 2012
A CAPSTONE IMPRINT
1710 ROE CREST DRIVE
NORTH MANKATO, MN 56003
WWW.CAPSTONEPUB.COM

CATALOGING-IN-PUBLICATION DATA IS AVAILABLE AT THE
LIBRARY OF CONGRESS WEBSITE.

ISBN: 978-1-4342-4090-3 (LIBRARY BINDING)
ISBN: 978-1-4342-4217-4 (PAPERBACK)

SUMMARY: AFTER BEING RELEASED FROM ARKHAM ASYLUM,
THE DARK KNIGHT'S MOST FRIGHTFUL FOE, THE SCARECROW,
SETS OUT TO CURE HIS ONE AND ONLY FEAR . . . BATS!
WITH A NEW AND IMPROVED FEAR TOXIN, HE'S GOING
AFTER ROBIN, BATMAN'S POWERFUL PARTNER. CAN THE BOY
WONDER OVERCOME SCARECROW'S SCARE TACTICS, OR WILL
HE BE SCARED TO DEATH?

ART DIRECTOR: BOB LENTZ
DESIGNER: BRANN GARVEY

PRINTED IN THE UNITED STATES OF AMERICA
IN STEVENS POINT, WISCONSIN.
032012   006678WZF12

TABLE OF CONTENTS

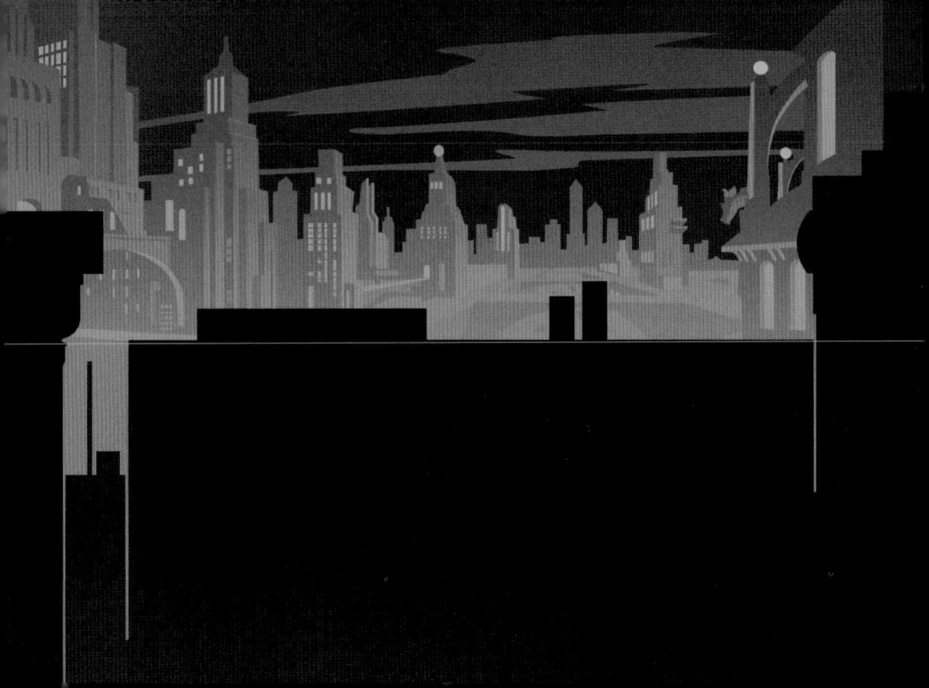

WHILE STILL A BOY, BRUCE WAYNE WITNESSED THE BRUTAL MURDER OF HIS PARENTS. THE TRAGIC EVENT CHANGED THE YOUNG BILLIONAIRE FOREVER. BRUCE VOWED TO RID GOTHAM CITY OF EVIL AND KEEP ITS PEOPLE SAFE FROM CRIME. AFTER YEARS OF TRAINING HIS BODY AND MIND, HE DONNED A NEW UNIFORM AND A NEW IDENTITY.

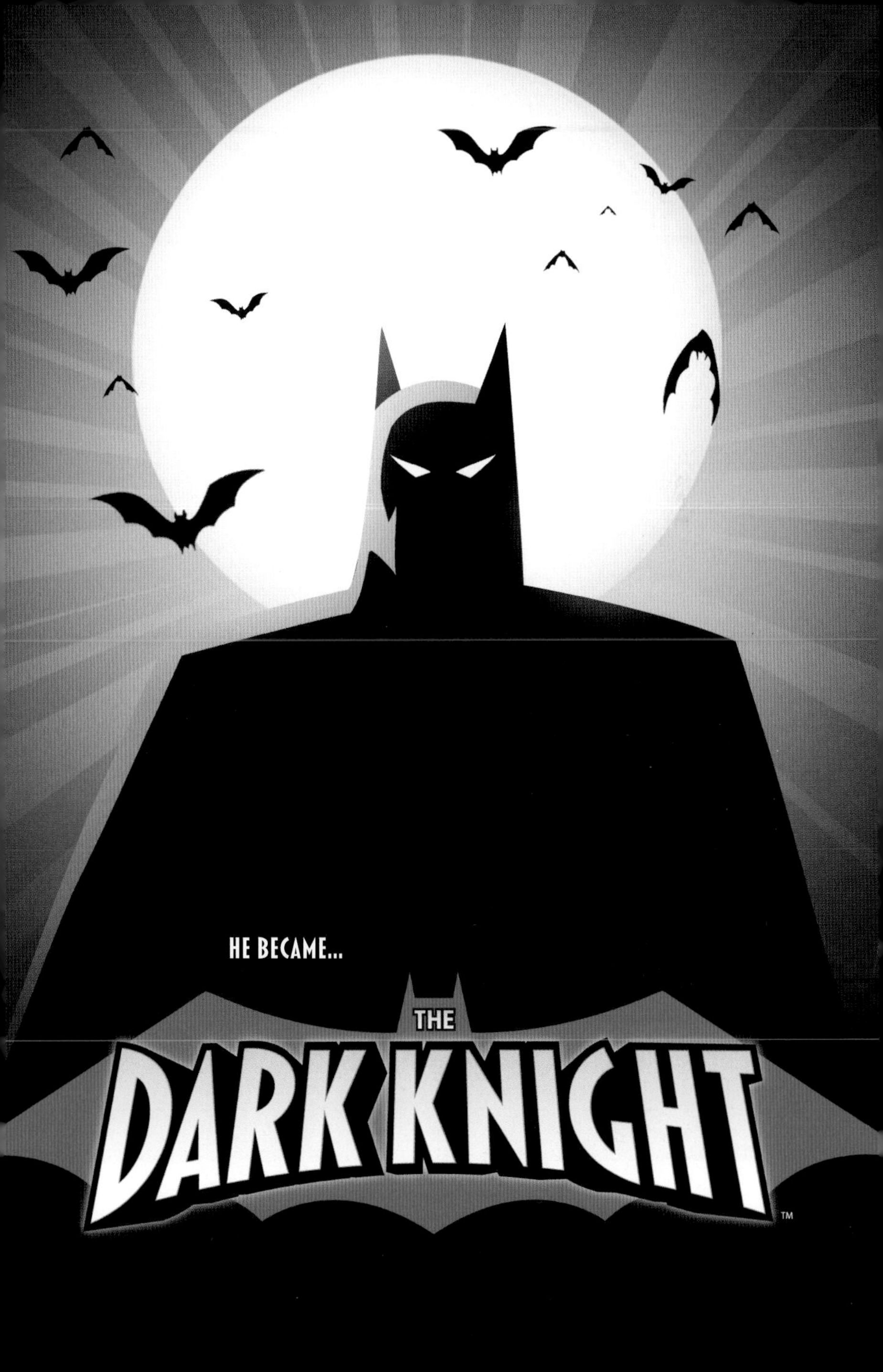
HE BECAME...
THE
DARK KNIGHT
TM

CHAPTER 1

THE CROW

Jonathan Crane couldn't run fast enough. No matter how hard he tried, he just couldn't seem to pick up his pace. It was almost like he was wading through deep water. His legs wouldn't do what his brain told them to do.

Behind him, Jonathan heard the caws of the crows. He looked over his shoulder. There were hundreds of them. They were as black as shadows. Their wings flapped violently.

The birds' sharp beaks glistened in the moonlight. Their jet black eyes were staring right at him. That was when Jonathan felt his foot catch on a rock on the cliff side.

THUDDDDD!

Jonathan fell to the ground. The crows would surely catch up to him now. He could see the swirling mass of birds flying closer and closer still. His heart pounded in his chest. The birds' wings flapped loudly in the air.

But the noise wasn't quite right. Crow wings didn't sound like that. Jonathan squinted at the approaching birds. And that was when he realized it.

They weren't crows at all. The mass of fluttering, flying beasts was actually a cloud of bats.

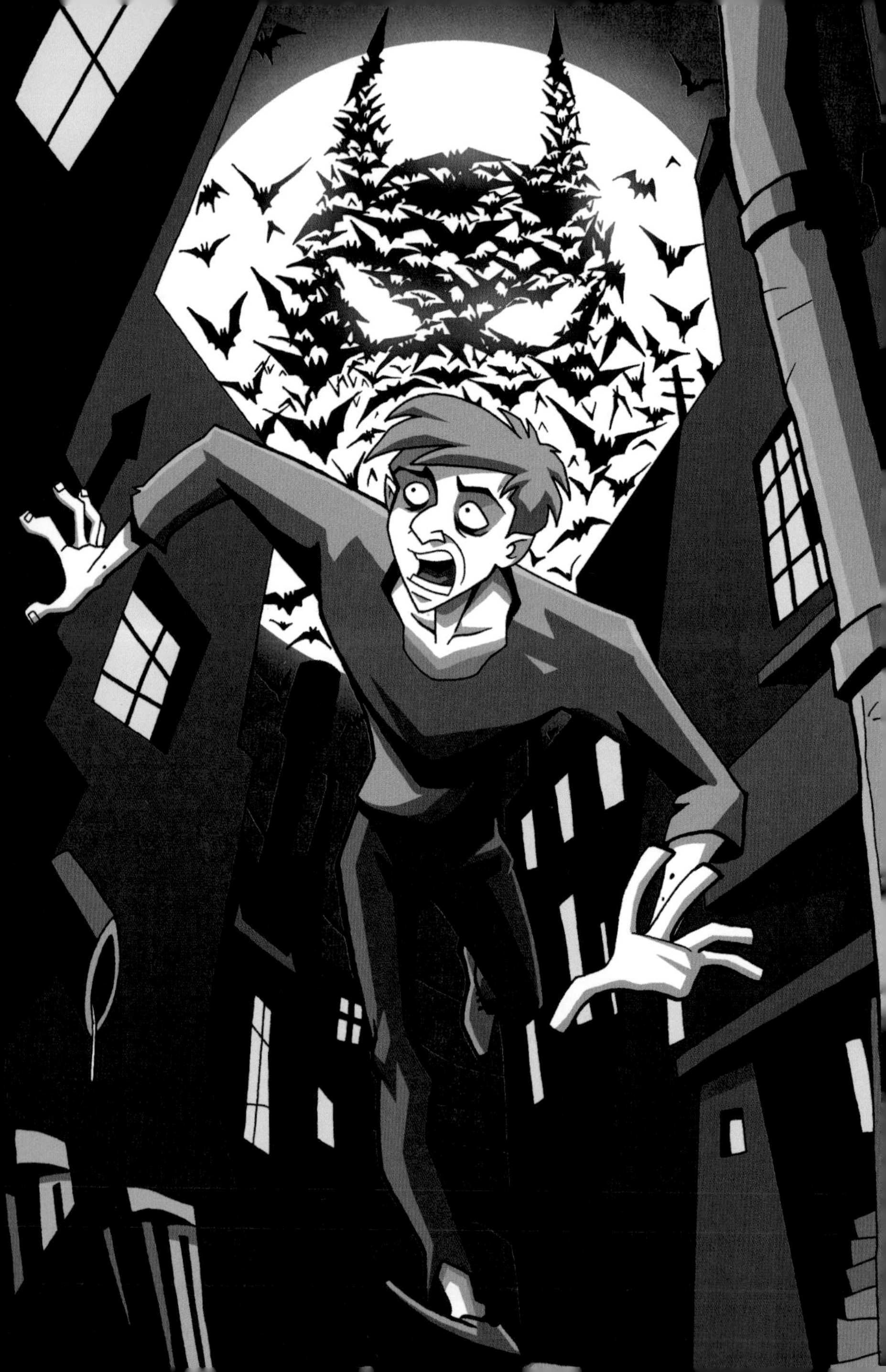

Jonathan got to his feet. The situation was worse than he thought. He stood up tall and looked down at his legs. They were skinny. He had always been a bit gangly. The kids in his high school had mocked him for his appearance. Even one of his college professors had made fun of him for his resemblance to a common scarecrow.

Jonathan narrowed his eyes. The bats were almost upon him. But he wasn't a helpless little boy any longer. He was a full-grown man. He would fight the creatures off. He wouldn't let them win.

There was a broom resting at his feet. Had this been what had tripped him? *No,* he thought. *That was a rock.* He had tripped on a rock. Hadn't he? Everything seemed so confusing now.

Jonathan saw that the broom was there, so he decided to pick it up and use it.

The first of the bats swooped down toward him. Jonathan Crane raised the broom and swung with all his might.

WOOOOOOOOSH!

The bat dodged his attack while another nipped at his ear from behind. Jonathan felt the fear rising in his chest again.
Two more bats swooped down at him. He swatted at them with his hands. But they were too quick. Suddenly, there were dozens of bats swarming all over him.

FLAP! FLAP! FLAP! FLAP! FLAP!

He tried to fight them off. There were just too many. The broom fell out of his hands to the ground below.

And then the rumbling started.

RUMMMMMMMMMMMMMMBLE!

It was a deep, primal sound coming from the darkness in front of him. He didn't want to look, but Jonathan couldn't help it. He had to see this beast that was approaching him. The sound grew louder. A hot gust of wind rushed out from the darkness. Jonathan knew it was the creature's breath. It had a foul smell to it. A smell like death.

The creature moved closer. Slowly, the beast stepped out from the shadows. Jonathan's heart pounded louder. Standing in front of him was a giant bat. It was like nothing he had ever seen before. Jonathan looked down at his clothing. Suddenly, he was wearing his Scarecrow costume.

But why wasn't it working?

When Jonathan was dressed like that, he was supposed to cause fear. He wasn't supposed to feel it himself.

The monster towered over the Scarecrow. The beast looked down and lowered its head toward him. The Scarecrow felt the air around him shift as the monster took in his scent.

ROOOOOAAAAARRR!

The creature let out a terrifying beliow. The Scarecrow cowered in front of it. He lowered himself to the ground and curled up into a little ball. It was what he had done when the crows had first attacked him all those years ago. Perhaps the position would save him now.

A full minute passed. Then Jonathan Crane opened his eyes. Maybe the horrible monster had gone away.

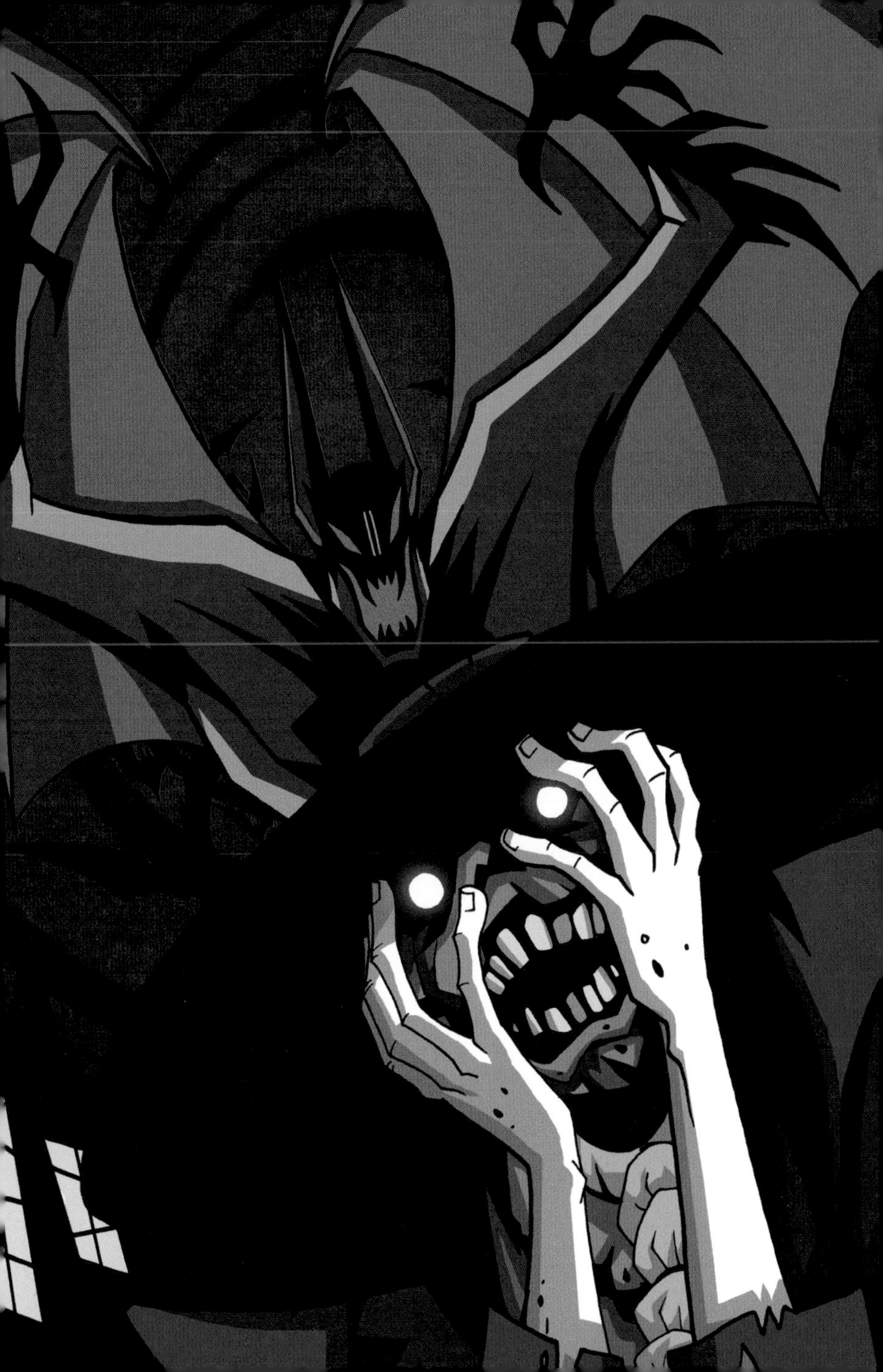

Jonathan stared upward. The monster hadn't moved. And now its mouth was open. Wide open. It was ready to feast. The creature inched closer. Jonathan screamed in terror.

AHHHHHHHHHHHHHHHHH!

And then Jonathan Crane woke up.

His nightmares were getting worse. This one had been particularly vivid. Jonathan stood up and shook his head. His heart was still beating rapidly. He was covered in sweat.

Jonathan walked toward the small window that was situated in the corner of his equally small hotel room. He pushed the window open and felt the cool, fall air of Gotham City rush in and brush against his face.

Jonathan knew what these dreams meant, of course. Before he had begun his career as the criminal known as the Scarecrow, Jonathan Crane had been a professor of psychology. He understood the way the human mind worked. He knew it was the Dark Knight who truly haunted his dreams.

As a boy, Jonathan had been terrified of crows. It was a childhood trauma that stayed with him even into his adult life. But now, his dreams always came back to bats — one giant bat in particular.

It hardly seemed fair. After all, it was because of Batman that Jonathan had any problems at all. Batman had stood in the way of his fear experiments. Just like the college board that fired him, Batman wouldn't allow Crane's experiments.

Batman called his tests "twisted" and "sick." He stood in the way of Jonathan mastering the art of fear. It was Batman's fault that the Scarecrow had been caged at Arkham Asylum.

Sure, Jonathan had broken a few laws. But it was all in the name of science. *It should be Batman whose dreams were haunted,* Crane thought. *Not my own.*

Jonathan had been paroled from Arkham now. He was a free man. So why did he feel like he was still in a jail cell? Batman should be the one trapped in a prison of his own thoughts.

Jonathan's mind reeled. He paced around his tiny hotel room. How could he frighten Batman? All his past attempts had failed miserably.

His mind thought back again to his own childhood fear. The crow. It was a terrifying creature. If only Batman was frightened of something similar from his own past. If only the Scarecrow could go back in time and scare Batman as a boy. A childhood trauma like that would surely stick with him. It would be the Scarecrow's face that Batman would see when he closed his eyes at night. It would be the Scarecrow's face that would make Batman go mad.

A smile slowly crept onto Jonathan's lips. Batman wasn't a boy now, that much was true. But his young partner was. Robin, the Boy Wonder. This fact was even part of his name. He was still just a boy. While it was too late to create a lifelong phobia in Batman's mind, Robin was the perfect age.

He would wait until the time was right.

Then the Scarecrow would terrify the Boy Wonder. He would haunt Robin's nightmares. And as a result, he would haunt Batman's dreams as well.

Jonathan Crane knew fear. He knew that, by hurting Robin, Batman would be plagued with guilt. He would blame himself for the Boy Wonder's suffering. He would find reasons to feel responsible. After all, the Dark Knight had trained the young hero. He had given Robin the tools and the knowledge to be a crime fighter. He had put him in harm's way.

Jonathan didn't agree with that logic, though. Batman would not be to blame for the Boy Wonder's misfortune. But if there's one thing Crane understood, it was the mind. And fear had the potential to make men lose perspective. All men.

Even Batman.

Jonathan Crane looked over at his Scarecrow costume that hung limply on a nearby chair. He smiled. The plan was too perfect, really. The Scarecrow would destroy both Batman and Robin in a single stroke.

He would destroy two birds with one stone.

CHAPTER 2

THE ROBIN

The Boy Wonder ducked. The metal pipe missed his head and collided with the wall behind him.

THWACK! The young hero sent an uppercut into the jaw of his attacker. The large man staggered backwards. He fell to the ground with a *THUD!*

Robin stood and looked around. All four of Roxy Rocket's men were lying on the ground unconscious. He glanced over at Batman. His partner didn't seem happy.

"I'm going after Roxy," Batman growled. He took his grapnel gun out of his belt and fired it toward the skyline.

ZIPPPPP!

The small grappling hook wrapped around a gargoyle on the rooftop of a nearby building. Robin reached into this own belt. "I'm going alone this time, Robin," said Batman. "It's late. You need to head back to the cave."

Robin was about to protest, but then he thought better of it. There was no use arguing with Batman when he had made up his mind. If he wanted to take on Roxy Rocket alone, then that's exactly what he was going to do. And Batman knew what he was doing. Even if it meant that Robin was stuck on cleanup detail.

"Don't forget to call it in," Batman said as he lifted up into the air. His grapnel pulled him toward the top of the nearby building.

Robin watched his partner disappear over the rooftop's ledge. Then he took a small device off of his belt and spoke into it. "We need a patrol car at the corner of First Avenue," he said. He pressed a button on the device and put it back on his belt.

The police would be here shortly. By now, they had learned to take calls from Batman and Robin seriously. Robin looked back at the men who were unconscious on the ground around him. They weren't going anywhere. He wasn't needed there any longer.

The Boy Wonder reached into this belt and found his own grapnel.

Robin fired it in the opposite direction of where Batman had headed. It wrapped around the leg of a rooftop water tower.

Suddenly, Robin felt something he couldn't explain. It was like someone was watching him. He looked over his shoulder at the alley behind him. All he saw were shadows. There wasn't anyone there. Or at least, Robin couldn't see anyone. *Weird,* he thought.

ZIPPPPPPPP! Robin pushed the Recoil button on the side of his grapnel. Wind rushed to meet him as he rose up into the air. It was a particular thrill Robin would never get tired of. It was the closest thing he would ever get to flying. The grapnel was definitely one of the perks of being Batman's partner.

THUMPPPPP!

Robin landed on the rooftop. It was time to head home — that's what Batman had said, anyway. Thankfully there were plenty of buildings between here and Wayne Manor. Robin wasn't quite ready to call it a night, so the jog would do him some good.

He placed the grapnel back on his belt and took a couple steps back toward the center of the rooftop. If he was going to make it to the next building, he would need a running start.

Suddenly, Robin felt that sensation again, like he was still being watched. He'd been getting that odd feeling for going on a week now. Robin looked over his shoulder. He couldn't see anyone. He shrugged. And then he started to run.

Eleven rooftops later, Robin stopped for a break.

Across the street was an old building. It had certainly seen better days. Robin had been told that back when Batman was young, the building had been a pretty fancy apartment complex. But time hadn't been kind to it. Now it was just another Gotham City eyesore. In fact, the building was so rundown, it was set for demolition. If Robin remembered correctly, the building was going to be torn down that very night.

Robin took a seat on the rooftop's ledge. He'd never seen a building be demolished before. He thought that it might be an interesting thing to witness.

As he watched a few workmen scurrying around on the street below, Robin felt a chill run through his body. He had that familiar eerie feeling yet again. He snapped his head around.

There was no one behind him. There was no one anywhere near him. All he could see were a large chimney and a whole lot of shadows.

Robin turned back around to face the building. He felt a little nervous. Maybe this wasn't such a good idea after all. Maybe he should just head home and call it a night.

Suddenly, he heard a rattling sound behind him. Robin turned to see a small capsule rolling across the rooftop. It came to a stop at the foot of the ledge. Robin bent down to inspect it.

FWOOOOOOSH!

Smoke erupted from all sides of the capsule. Some kind of strange green gas was spraying out of it.

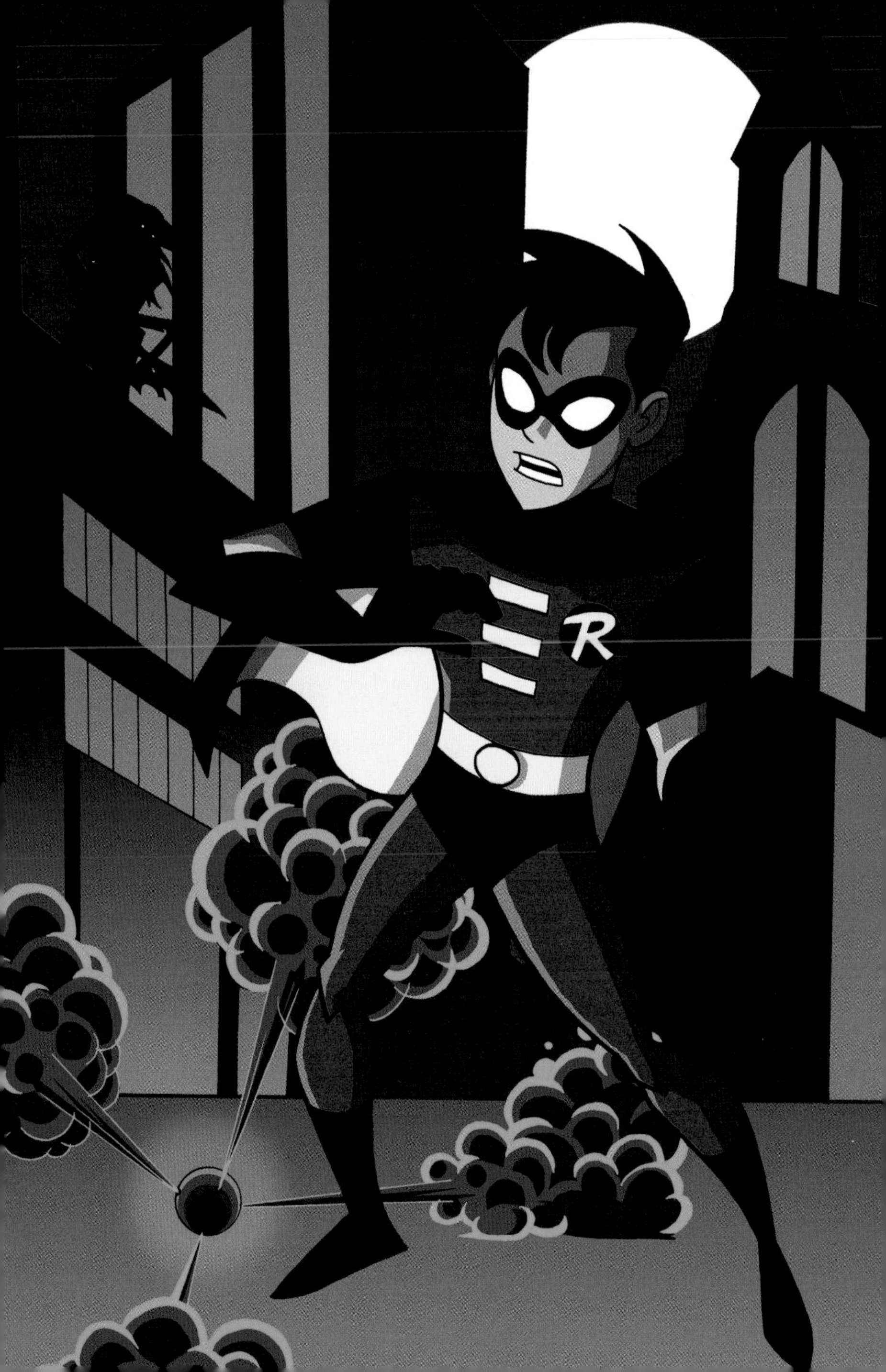

Robin straightened and tried to back up, but it was too late. He had already breathed in a large amount of the gas. Robin staggered to his feet. He leaned on the ledge for support.

"Terrible thing, isn't it?" said a voice. It seemed to be coming from the shadows behind the chimney. "Fear, I mean." The Scarecrow stepped out into the light of the full moon. Even with his mask mostly hidden by the brim of his hat, he was more frightening than Robin remembered.

"Scarecrow," Robin said.

"That's right, boy," the criminal said. He walked over toward Robin. "Scarecrow. It's a name you'll remember from now on, I think. It's something you'll see in your dreams every night when you go to sleep."

"No!" screamed Robin. It came out much louder than he had intended.

"The Scarecrow will haunt you, Boy Wonder," the Scarecrow said. "I will haunt you every night for the rest of your life. Do you feel your heart racing? The sweat beading on your forehead? Your mind knows it's just your body's reaction to my fear gas. But you're still just as afraid."

With every word, Robin's head seemed to grow more and more pinched. He couldn't focus. He shook his head, but it was no use. The more the Scarecrow spoke, the more uneasy he felt.

Robin realized he had to act, and fast. In a matter of moments, the fear from the Scarecrow's gas would overwhelm him. *WOOOOOOOOOOOOOOOSH!* He lunged at the Scarecrow.

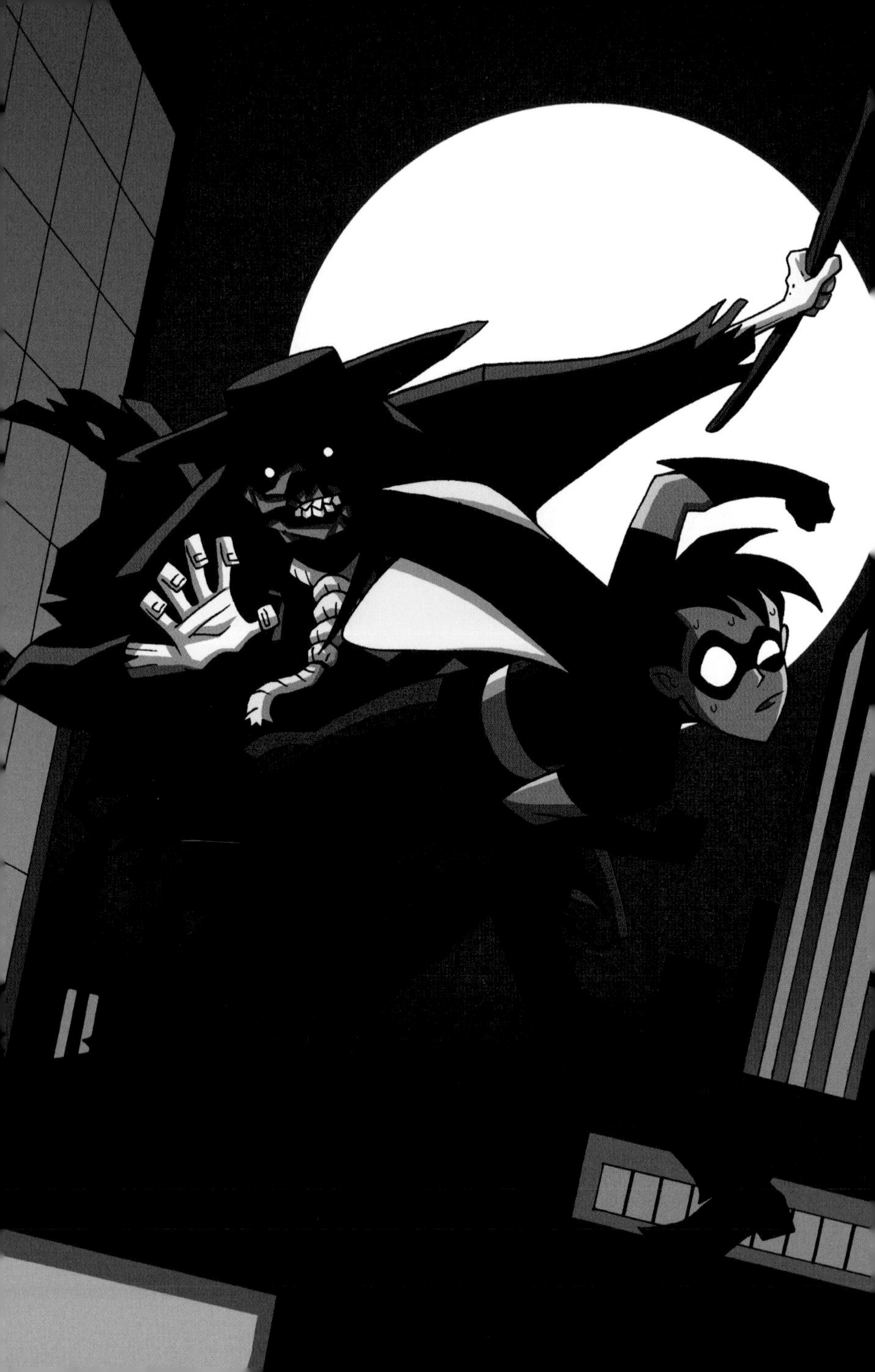

The Scarecrow easily evaded the attack. Robin was spooked, and his attacks weren't as quick or powerful as they normally were. The fear had already begun to take hold of his mind.

Robin lashed out again with a left punch, but the Scarecrow nimbly shifted his weight and deflected the punch with his forearm. The hero lost his balance and fell onto the rooftop with a *THUDDD!*

Robin rolled to his back in a panic. He knew he couldn't take on the Scarecrow in this state. He had to calm down and focus. He had to control his fear, as his mentor the Dark Knight had shown him time and time again. But all Robin could feel was numbing terror.

Fight it, the Boy Wonder told himself. *Fight the fear!*

As if he was reading Robin's thoughts, the Scarecrow spoke up. "It won't go away," he said. "You're not going to feel any better. The Scarecrow has crippled you with fear. There's no escape. And that's how you'll stay for the rest of your life."

"NO!" Robin screamed again. It was even louder than before.

Run! Robin heard himself think. *Run for your life!*

The Boy Wonder turned his back on the Scarecrow. He pulled out his grapnel and shot it away from the rooftop.

CLINK! The line caught hold of the top ledge of the old building. Robin pushed the Recoil button. **WOOOOOOOOOSH!** He shot away into the night air.

The Scarecrow walked slowly over to the rooftop's edge. He watched as Robin swung into one of the open windows of the rundown old building. The boy disappeared inside it, but the Scarecrow knew there was nowhere for him to hide. No matter how far he ran, the boy's fear would always haunt him.

KABOOOOOOM! The Scarecrow stared in amazement. The entire building was crumbling to the ground.

RUMMMMMMMMMMBLE!

The building was being demolished before the Scarecrow's very eyes. The walls broke into pieces. Dust clouds rose up from the base. The entire structure collapsed like a concrete accordion.

And Robin was trapped inside.

The villain took a step back on the rooftop. He hadn't planned for this to happen. He hadn't intended to kill the Boy Wonder.

Then the Scarecrow smiled. Then, slowly, his maniacal laugh rang out through Gotham's city streets.

HAHAHAHAHAHAHAHAHAHAH!

This might work out even better than my original plan, he thought. *Batman's young partner is dead, and I, the Scarecrow, am to blame. Perhaps this is an even better way to haunt the Caped Crusader's dreams!*

The Scarecrow turned and walked toward the building's rooftop exit. For the first time in months, his mind felt calm. He was in a rare good mood.

Mostly, the Scarecrow was looking forward to heading back to his small room at his hotel. Maybe tonight he would finally get a decent night's sleep.

A sleep without nightmares.

CHAPTER 3

THE CATBIRD

The Scarecrow looked through his
binoculars.

FLAP! FLAP! FLAP!

The wind from the rooftop whipped
through his coat. But the cold didn't bother
him. The Scarecrow was comfortable up
there on the water tower's catwalk.

The Scarecrow had always thought of
fall as his favorite season. Not just because
of Halloween. No, a little chill in the air
was good for a person now and again.

A little cold made you feel alive. It was like fear in that way. Not everyone liked feeling cold, but it sure did make you appreciate warmer weather.

Through the binoculars, the Scarecrow could see Commissioner James Gordon quite clearly. The man had been standing there for some time now. Gordon had come out onto the rooftop of police headquarters nearly half an hour ago. He had switched on the Bat-Signal and then just waited. He was hoping for Batman to come and fill him in on the Roxy Rocket case, no doubt.

But the Scarecrow didn't think that Batman was coming at all. The Dark Knight was probably back at his home, mourning the loss of his partner. The fall of Robin, the Boy Wonder.

"That would surely help Batman realize his greatest fear," the Scarecrow said to himself. He smiled at the thought of Batman being lost in misery.

The Scarecrow zoomed in on Gordon again. He looked impatient up there all alone, without the company of the Dark Knight. Maybe even lonely. Maybe afraid.

Gordon had better get used to it, the Scarecrow thought. *This was what his life would be like now. Gotham City would be without a Batman. And Gordon would be without his greatest asset in the war against crime.*

THUMP! A noise came from the rooftop. The Scarecrow fixed his binoculars. Something has just landed on top of police headquarters.

The building was blocking the Scarecrow's view. He couldn't quite tell what had been dropped on the roof. He slowly adjusted the zoom.

When the image finally came into focus, the Scarecrow didn't know what to think at first. The thing that had fallen onto the police's roof wasn't a thing at all. It was a woman. She was tied up in a thick cord. It was the kind of cord that Batman often used. And to make matters worse, the Scarecrow recognized the woman.

She was Roxy Rocket, the criminal the Dark Knight had been chasing last night. Despite what had happened to Robin, Batman was already back on patrol.

That can't be right, the Scarecrow thought. He focused his binoculars on Gordon.

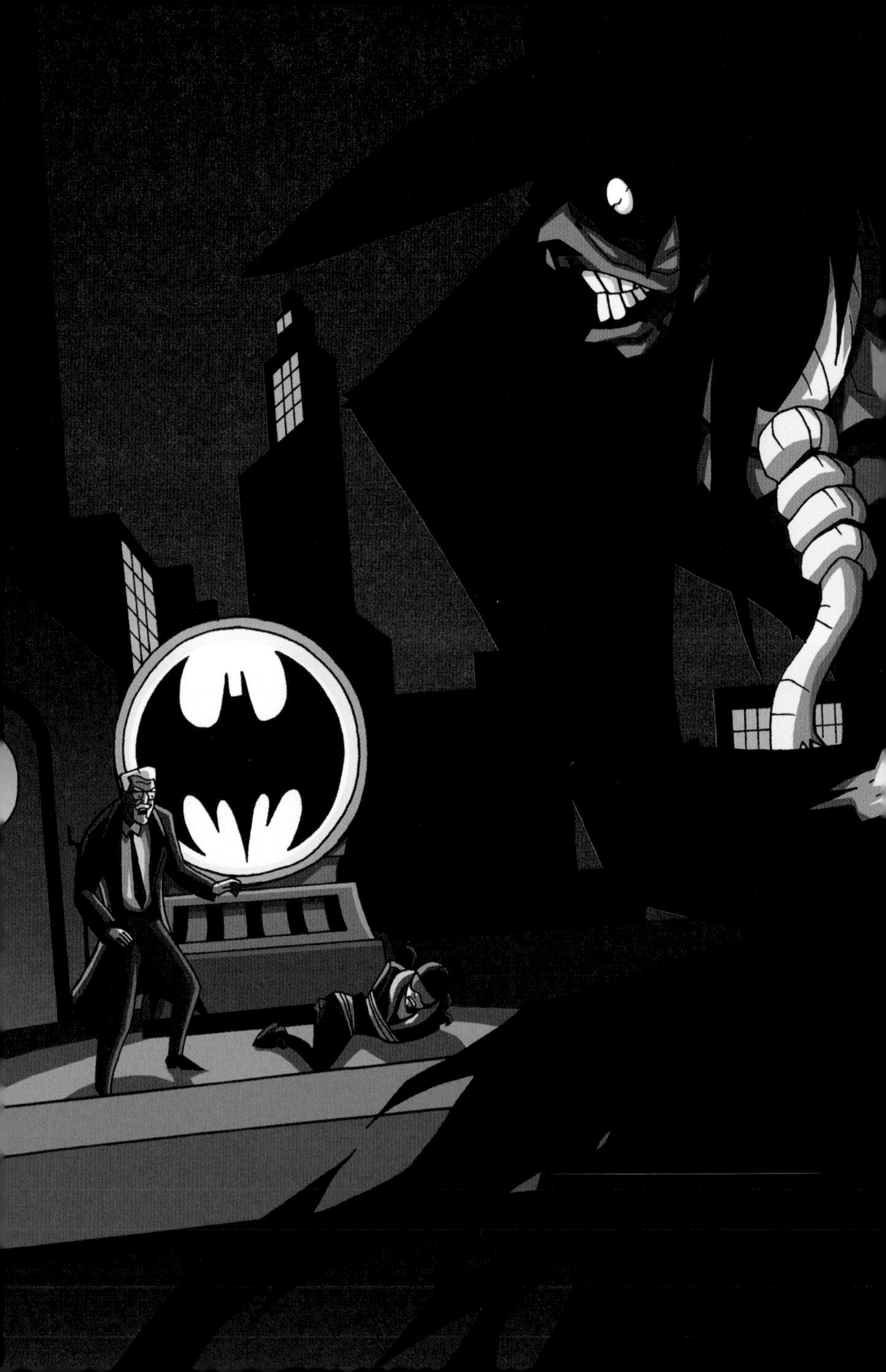

The Commissioner seemed surprised as well. He was looking around the rooftop for Batman. Apparently, the crime fighter hadn't felt the need to stop and chat. He had just dropped Roxy off and continued on his way. It was like he was too busy to take a break. Or maybe he was just too upset . . .

The Scarecrow stood up on the water tower's catwalk. He couldn't help but wonder if he had created a monster. Maybe Batman wasn't afraid of him at all. Maybe it was just the opposite.

Or maybe Batman was more dedicated to his job than ever, the Scarecrow thought. *That would definitely be a nightmare.*

But that couldn't be the case. No matter how tough and how strong the Dark Knight was, losing his partner would take its toll.

Yes, Batman would be miserable now. And scared. Frightened. A grim smile crept up the Scarecrow's face. *Perhaps even frightened to death,* he thought.

CRRRRRRRRRRRREAK!

The Scarecrow's thoughts were interrupted by a sound behind him. He spun around, fists raised, to face the source of the noise.

Nothing.

He slowly walked around the catwalk, but there was no one else up there.

It must have just been the sound of the water tower shifting in the breeze, the Scarecrow thought.

But when he looked around, he saw that no one was around.

The Scarecrow was quite alone. Worse still, he was cold.

And afraid.

CHAPTER 4

THE MOCKINGBIRD

The Scarecrow stood in the doorway to the diner and scanned it with his eyes. The room was full of men he recognized. They were second and third-rate crooks always up for a bit of dishonest work.

"I'm looking for a few able-bodied assistants," said the Scarecrow.

But for some reason, none of them looked up at him. They were all staring off at each other or back down at their drinks. No one was speaking. In fact, the entire room was strangely quiet.

The Scarecrow walked over to the counter. Behind him, he could hear a few of the men in the diner getting up and walking toward the exit.

"I need a few new hires," the Scarecrow said to the waiter. "Some men with a talent for crime."

The waiter ignored him. He turned away from the criminal. He started to dry a glass that had been resting on the sink's edge.

"Perhaps you didn't hear me," said the Scarecrow.

Again, the waiter didn't answer. He placed the dry glass on the counter. Then he picked up a wet mug. He began to wipe it down with his cloth.

The Scarecrow was dumbfounded. This had never happened before.

Whenever the Scarecrow opened his mouth, people listened. They were afraid what would happen to them if they didn't. In fact, the Scarecrow had never witnessed such disrespect since before he had ever donned his frightful costume.

"Who are you to ignore me?" he said in a slow and drawn out manner. Then he raised his hand toward the waiter.

HISSSSSSSSSSSSSSS!

A puff of green gas shot out from the Scarecrow's cuff and into the waiter's face.

"What are you doing?!" cried the waiter.

"So you can speak after all," said the Scarecrow.

"Spi — spiders!" the man said.

The waiter dropped down to the floor in a panic. He began scratching at his arms and legs.

"Arachnophobia? How cliché," said the Scarecrow. "You could have at least come up with an original fear. Next time, try to put a little more effort into it."

Behind him, the Scarecrow could hear the diner's door opening. From the sound of it, dozens of the men were exiting in a hurry.

"Let me ask you a question," said the Scarecrow. "Any idea of why these men aren't seeking my gainful employment? It's a little ungrateful, honestly. Usually, a criminal's skin crawls with excitement and fear whenever I ask them to help."

"Spiders!" said the waiter.

The man was obviously having trouble concentrating. The Scarecrow's fear gas was making him live out his worst nightmares.

"Yes, yes, spiders. They're crawling all over you," said the Scarecrow. He sounded quite bored. "But try to concentrate, would you? I asked you a question, and I expect an answer."

"It's . . . it's Batman," said the waiter. "Ever since his partner, Robin, died, he's been — he's been coming down on us harder than normal."

The man twitched with fear. He scratched at invisible spiders crawling over his skin. "Everybody knows it was you who killed him," the man said with wide eyes. "You killed Robin! That's . . . that's too horrible. Even for this crowd."

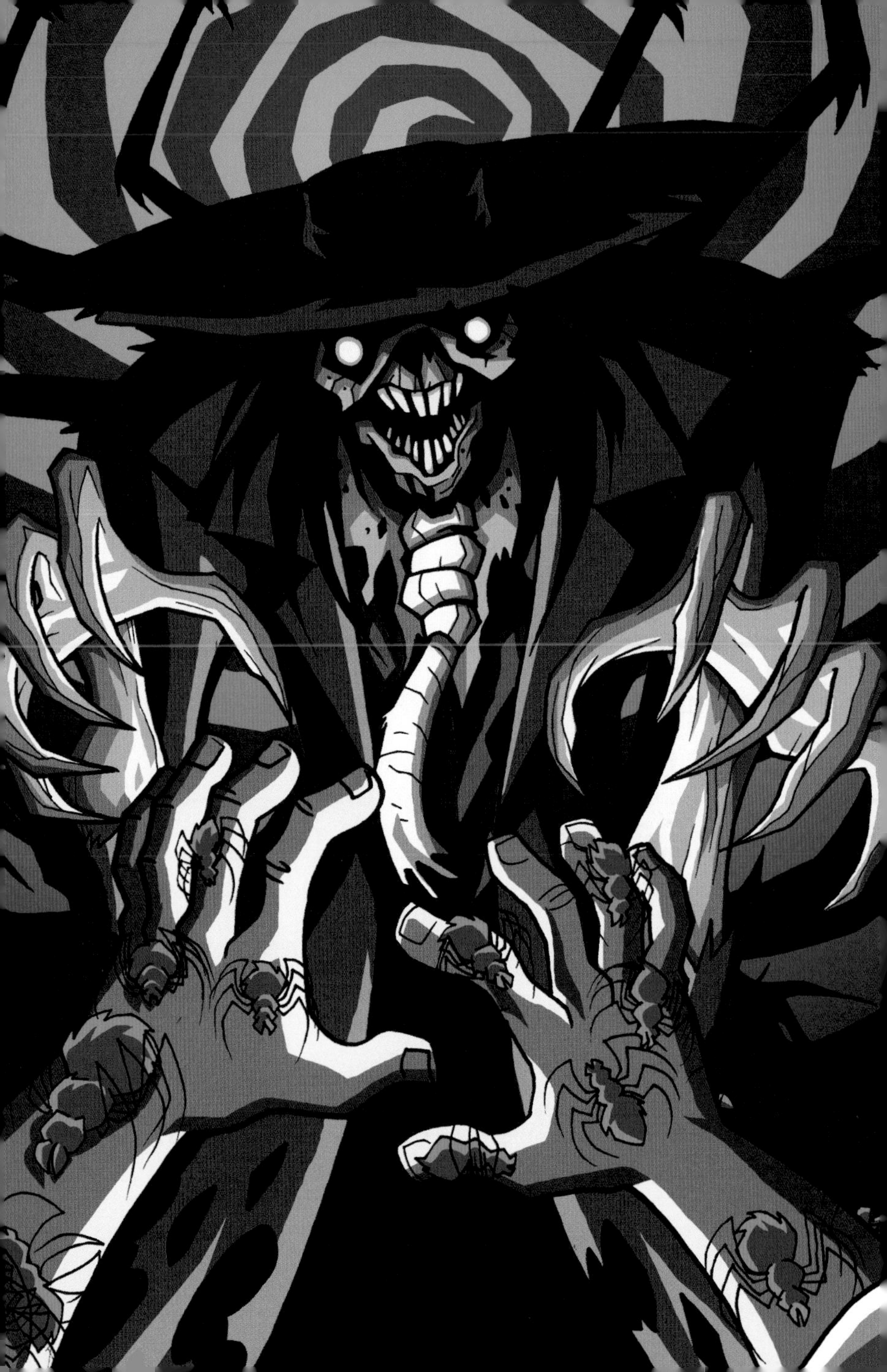

The Scarecrow turned away from the diner. "Pathetic," he said. "Not a backbone in the whole lot of you. You're all just a bunch of cowards."

No one answered. But the Scarecrow didn't expect them to. There was hardly anyone left in the diner. Only a few men had stuck around to finish their drinks.

"Please! Please," the waiter said from behind the counter. "Get them away from me, please . . . the spiders are everywhere!"

But the Scarecrow had learned what he'd wanted to know. He walked away from the counter and out the diner's door.

Maybe next time, the waiter would remember not to disrespect the Scarecrow. But the villain hoped that wouldn't be the case. He truly loved using his fear gas.

The Scarecrow loved fear. Even his own fear thrilled and chilled him. Many people thought he was immune to fear like he was to his fear gas. But that simply wasn't the case. He accepted fear for what it was. He embraced it. It made him strong.

The Scarecrow turned a corner and started walking down a dimly lit alley. His hotel was only a few blocks from there. The night air was so refreshing to him. It seemed like the perfect evening for a walk.

Halfway down the alley, the Scarecrow heard footsteps coming from behind him.

TAP TAP TAP TAP!

The Scarecrow turned around just in time to see a shadowy figure leap up to the fire escape on a nearby building. The shape of the figure looked like a boy.

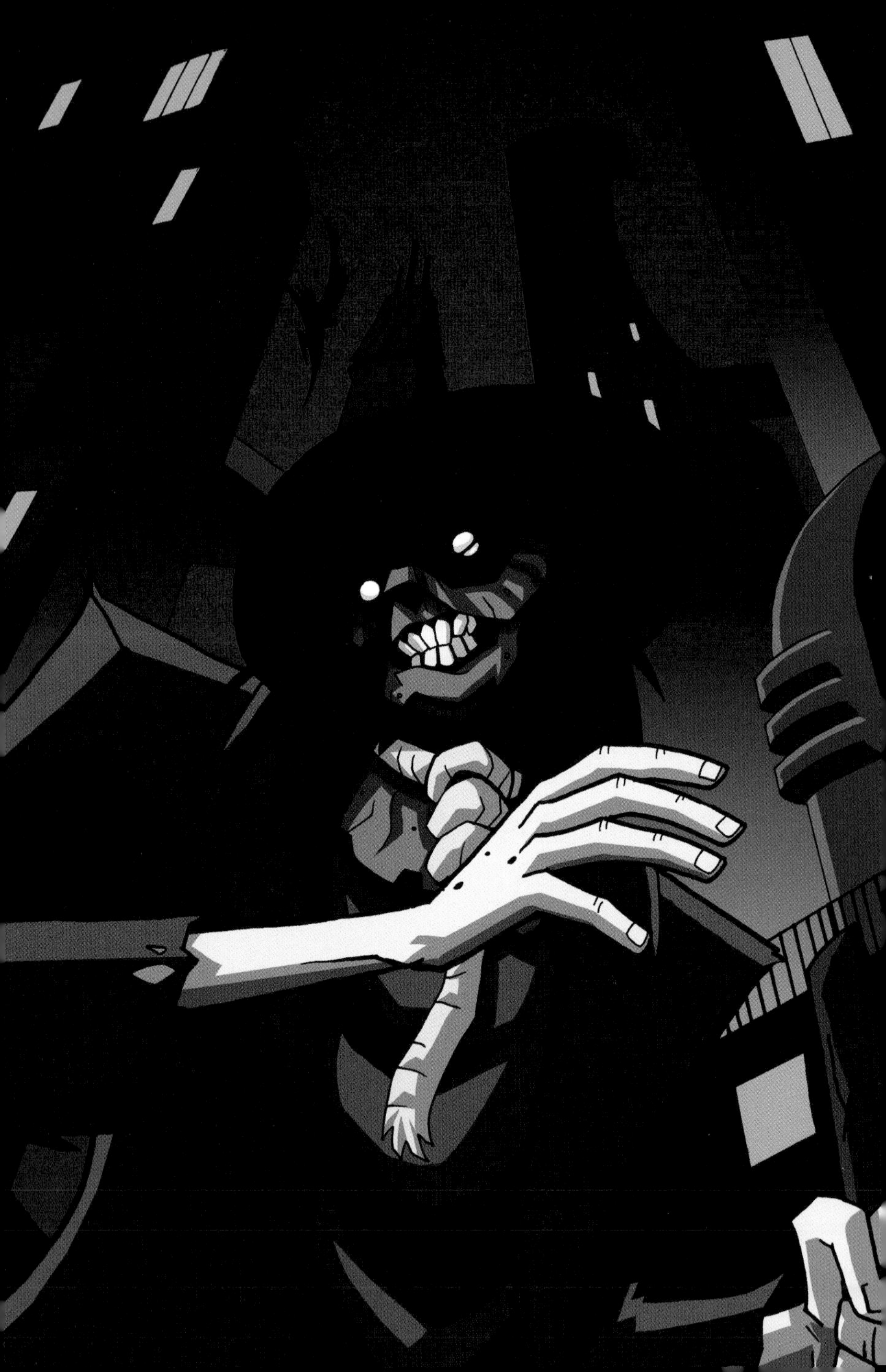

The Scarecrow watched as the figure raced up the fire escape and became lost in the shadows of the building's rooftop.

The way he moved, the Scarecrow thought. *It was just like . . .*

But that was impossible. Robin was gone. Dead. The Scarecrow's eyes must be playing tricks on him.

Perhaps I'm not as immune to my own fear gas as I had thought, he wondered. It was possible that, over time, the fear gas was building up in his system. Perhaps now it was starting to affect him after years of inhaling second-hand fumes.

That might require some looking into, the Scarecrow thought.

He turned back around and continued on toward his hotel.

HAHAHAHAHAHAHAHAHAHA!

As the Scarecrow walked, he thought he heard the sound of mocking laughter coming from the rooftops. The noise was muffled, so he couldn't be sure that was what he was hearing. But either way, the Scarecrow started to walk a bit faster.

And this time, he didn't look back.

CHAPTER 5

NEVERMORE

CLICK! CLICKKKK!

The lock on the door took a little bit of work. But finally, the Scarecrow managed to jimmy it open.

CRREEAAAAAAAAAAAK! He walked through the doorway, looking carefully around the room. It was too dark to see anything clearly. But nevertheless, he didn't dare turn on a light. The Scarecrow had already had enough trouble with the two guards downstairs. He didn't need to attract any more unwanted attention.

As if on cue, a bright light shone in the Scarecrow's face. Standing behind him in the hall was yet another guard. The Scarecrow was annoyed. How many guards did this chemical plant have?

"Who — who are you?" demanded the guard. It was hard to tell with the light shining in his face, but the Scarecrow was pretty sure the man was shaking. The Scarecrow's costume often got that result.

"Do you really have to ask?" said the Scarecrow as he took another step toward the guard.

"Stop right there!" yelled the guard. But the Scarecrow took yet another step forward. The guard took his heavy flashlight and swung it at the villain.

WOOOOOOOOOOSH!

The Scarecrow ducked out of the way just as the flashlight swung over his head.

The Scarecrow reached out his arms. Two quick puffs shot out from the villain's wrists.

POOF! POOF

The guard turned away. But he had already inhaled the green gas.

"Y-you," he started to say. Then he dropped his flashlight to the ground.

CRUNCH!

The flashlight's lens shattered as it hit the hard tile floor. It took a few minutes, but the Scarecrow's eyes slowly adjusted to the darkness. When he could finally see again, he noticed that the guard was facing away from him, toward the hallway's wall.

The man was holding his knees as he sat on the ground. The terrified guard was shaking his head back and forth, as if silently saying "no" over and over. The sight was beautiful to the Scarecrow. This was the kind of thing he lived for.

The Scarecrow noticed the man's shattered flashlight.

That's a shame, the criminal thought. He hadn't remembered to bring his own flashlight with him. That was the sort of thing reserved for henchmen to think of.

That was just another reason he hated doing this sort of work by himself. It had been years since he had been forced to break into a chemical factory to steal supplies. It seemed so beneath him.

But now that Batman had every hood in town terrified, the Scarecrow didn't have much of a choice. He had to get his own hands dirty.

To make matters worse, the Scarecrow was sure that Batman was currently staking out chemical plants. It would be the first thing the Caped Crusader would do if he was as angry as the waiter had said. Batman would know that the Scarecrow needed chemicals to create his fear gas. He would probably assume that the villain's supply was low by now. And that would mean he would be on the prowl.

And there were only three such factories inside Gotham's city borders. What the Scarecrow was doing that night was risky.

Nevertheless, the villain walked away from the guard and back into the nearby room. In the corner stood a large safe. It held some of the rare ingredients the Scarecrow needed. He walked over to it.

The Scarecrow pulled a glass vial out of his pocket. He unscrewed the vial's lid and poured its contents onto the safe's latch. Smoke began to rise from the lock as the acid ate away at the safe's steel exterior. After a minute, the safe's door popped open. At least that part was easier than the Scarecrow had remembered.

The Scarecrow pulled open the safe's door even wider. He strained to see inside it. It was too dark for him to get a good idea of what he was looking at. He reached into his pocket and pulled out a matchbook. He tore one away.

Crane had taken the little book from his hotel's front desk. He always kept a few on him, for the Scarecrow loved fire.

Which is rather odd, the Scarecrow thought with a smile. *Scarecrows are supposed to be afraid of fire.*

SCRATCCCCCCCCCH!

The Scarecrow lit a match, and peered again inside the safe. It took the criminal two minutes and seven matches to find what he was looking for.

But finally, a set of eight test tubes hanging in a wooden stand caught his eye.

After reading a few of the labels, the Scarecrow leaned out of the safe. He stood up straight again. He held the test tubes tightly in his hand and smiled under his mask.

So far, this little heist wasn't as difficult as he had imagined it would be.

The Scarecrow's mind began to drift as he walked out of the room. He was already thinking about setting up his workspace back at the hotel. He was deciding what beakers he would need and where he would get some of the more common ingredients for his next batch of fear gas. He was so lost in thought, in fact, that it took him a few moments to realize that there was someone standing at the other end of the hallway.

There in the shadows stood a small figure. It wasn't the guard. He was still sitting quietly on the floor by the open door. The Scarecrow couldn't make out the figure's face. But he knew exactly who he was staring at.

"You're not real!" the Scarecrow shouted suddenly.

The small figure in the shadows didn't respond.

"You're a result of the fear gas I sprayed on the guard," said the Scarecrow. He was talking in a quieter voice now. He was trying to calm himself down. "You're just some side effect I haven't worked out yet. That's all you are and nothing more."

The figure stayed silent.

"I killed you," said the Scarecrow. "You're dead. Robin is dead."

The shadow didn't say a thing. It didn't even move. "You think you can win?" said the Scarecrow. "Well you can't!"

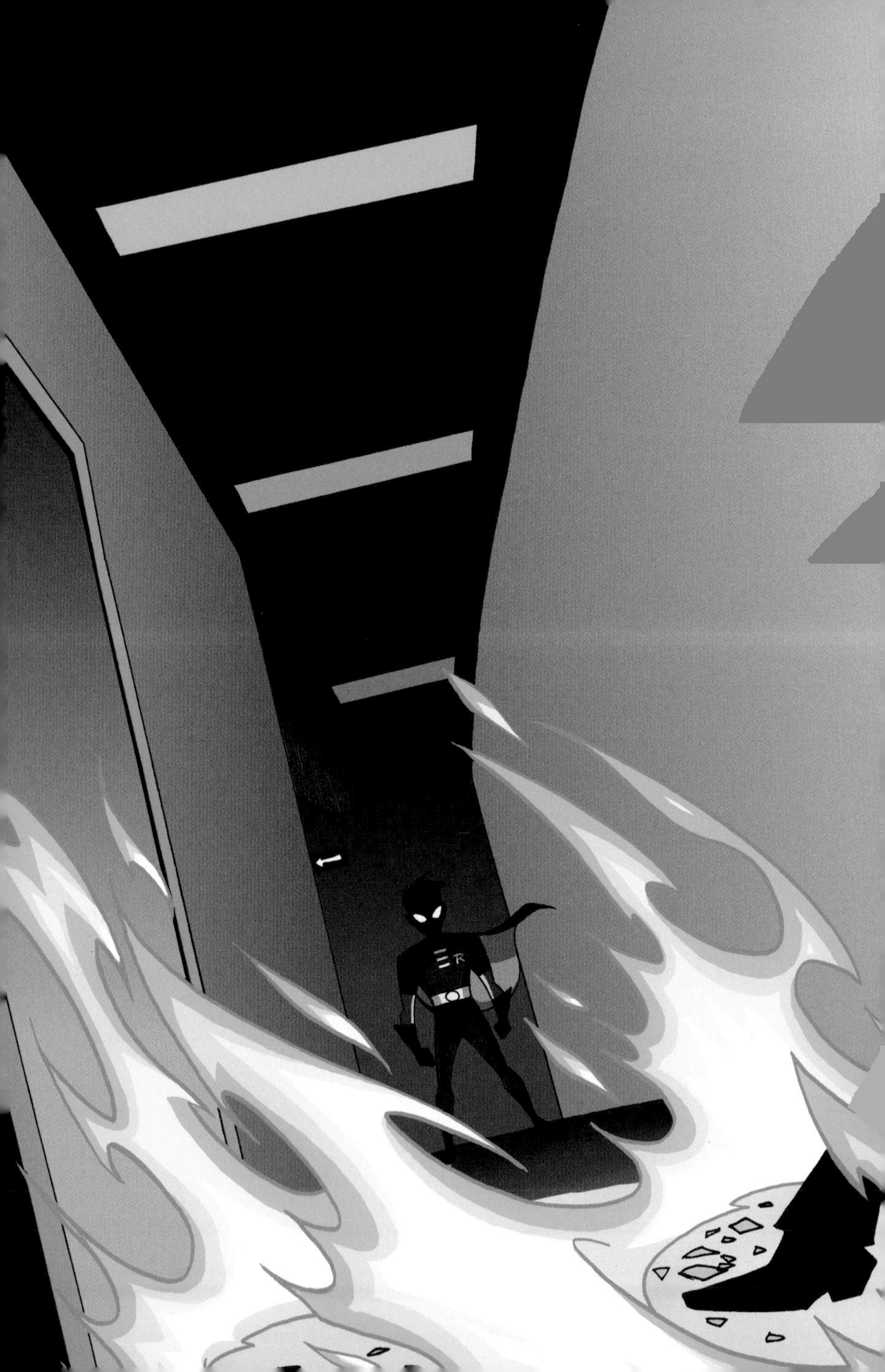

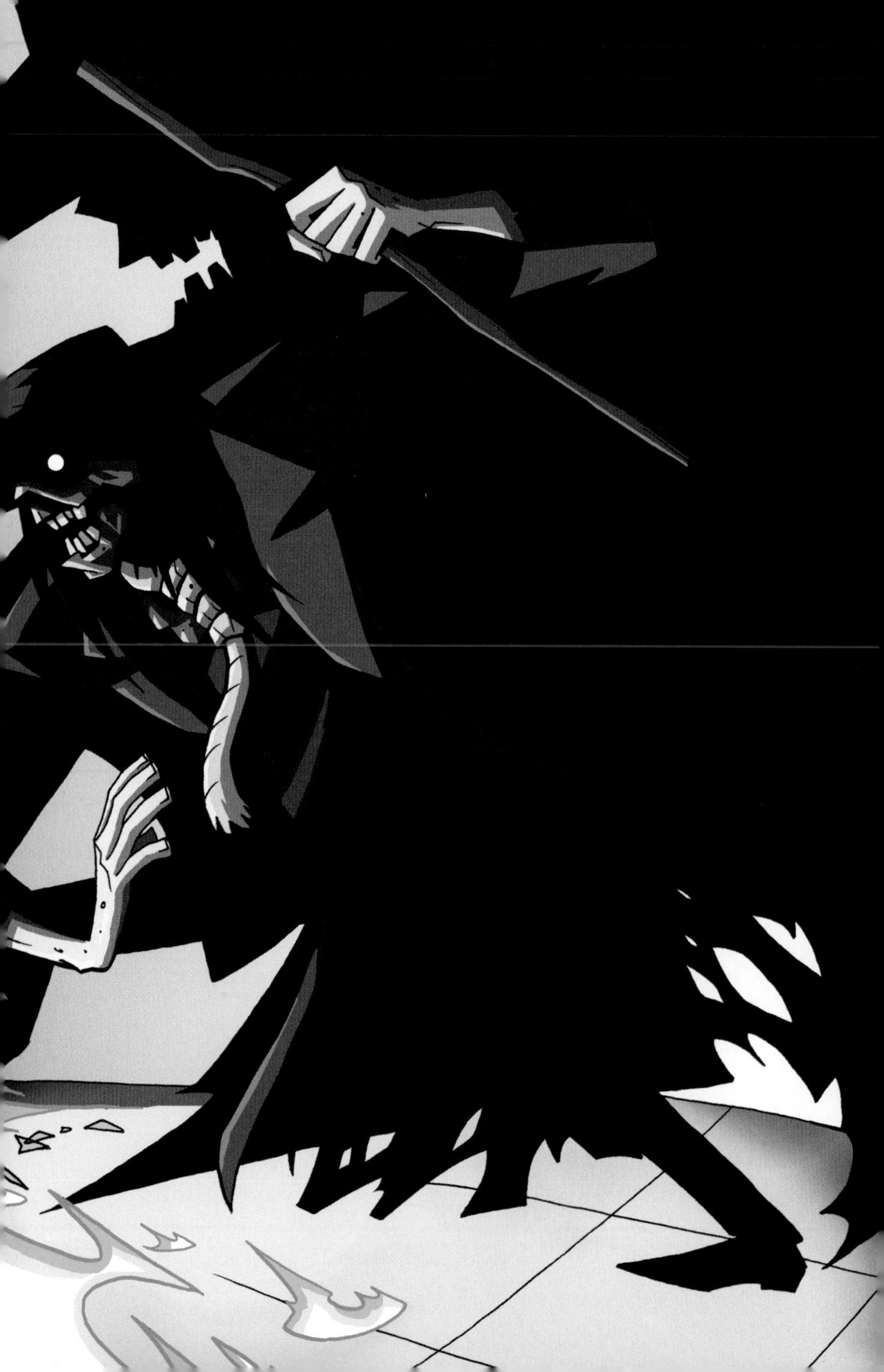

The Scarecrow sounded even crazier than usual. He threw his test tubes down on the hallway's floor.

KIRSSSSHHH!

The glass tubes smashed against the tile near the shadow's feet. The shadow still didn't respond. In fact, it stayed perfectly still.

Then the Scarecrow pulled his matchbook out of his pocket. He lit a match and hurled it at the shadow. His matchbook fell to the ground.

FWOOOOM!

As the match hit the tile, the spilt chemicals burst into flames. With the fire burning behind him, Scarecrow ran toward the opposite end of the hall, shrieking in fear.

The Scarecrow pushed open the door to the stairwell and hurried down the dark staircase. Behind him, the shadowy figure stepped out of the darkness and across the already dimming fire.

The figure walked over to the where the Scarecrow had been standing. The shadow person bent down to pick something up off the floor. In his gloved hands was the matchbook the Scarecrow had dropped.

He flipped it closed to see the logo on its cover. "The Royal Hotel," he read aloud. "1941 South Elm Street."

*   *   *

All Jonathan Crane wanted to do was sleep. But that was proving a bit difficult on that particular night. He slept fitfully, if at all, between nightmares.

It had been hours since he returned home from the chemical factory. But Jonathan wasn't feeling any calmer.

Had he actually seen the ghost of Robin? Maybe it was just a peculiar shadow in the hallway. The figure hadn't moved, after all. Or had it? Jonathan couldn't be sure of anything anymore.

Crane looked down at his hands. He clutched the blanket on his bed tightly. His fists looked pale in the darkness. The moon's light was creeping in through the closed blind on the window. The light gave everything an eerie glow.

The hotel was already a bit depressing and rundown in the daylight. But in the light of the full moon, it seemed spookier and otherworldly.

Crane regretted getting a room in that particular hotel now. But he was regretting a lot of things lately.

CRRRRRRRRREAK!

The floorboard over by his closet creaked quietly. Jonathan peered over at it. His heart nearly beat out of his chest. For a second, he thought there was a man standing in the corner of his room. But it was just his Scarecrow costume, draped over its usual chair.

TAP! TAP! TAP!

Jonathan heard a sound at the window. He snapped his head over to look at it. The sound stopped. There was nothing there. All he could see was the full moon and the blood red sky of the Gotham night.

SCRATCH! SCRATCH!

There was sound coming from under Jonathan's bed. He swallowed nervously. Then he summoned all the courage he had left. He swung his head over the side of his mattress. There was nothing under his bed — just a few dust bunnies and scraps of paper.

CRRRRRRRRREAK!

Jonathan looked again at his closet. His pulse raced. There was still no one there.

SCRATCH! SCRATCH!

There was the sound under his bed again. Jonathan stayed perfectly still. It was nothing, he told himself. He didn't need to check. There was nothing there.

TAP! TAP! TAP!

And there was the noise at the window again.

Jonathan couldn't make himself look. He closed his eyes.

TAP! TAP! TAP!

Why was this happening to him? Why was he being haunted? He hadn't wanted the boy to die. It was an accident.

TAP! TAP! TAP!

Crane couldn't take it anymore. He leapt out of his bed and onto the floor. He didn't even bother to grab his shoes or pants. He ran out into the hall wearing only his nightshirt. He just had to get out of that room.

WHAM!

Suddenly, Jonathan was lying on the ground. His face hurt. What had he run into? He looked up . . . and saw Batman standing over him!

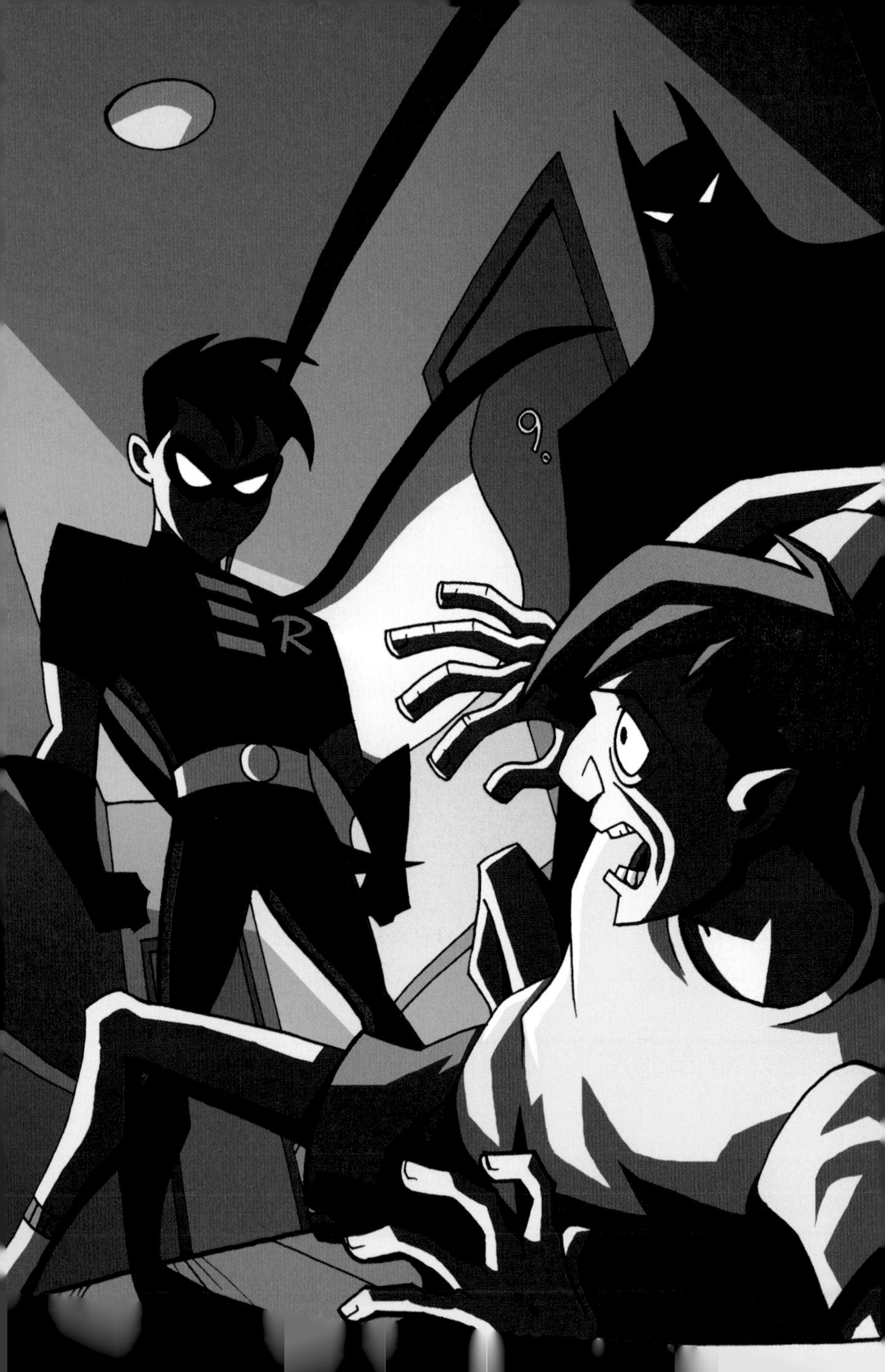
9.

"No!" Jonathan screamed. He got to his feet and turned toward the other end of the hall.

Crane froze in his tracks. There in the shadows in front of him stood Robin. There was no doubt about it. The boy wasn't hidden in shadows this time. He wasn't disappearing over rooftops. The ghost of Robin the Boy Wonder was standing just a few feet away from Jonathan Crane. And he looked very angry.

It was all too much for Crane. He felt like he had as a boy when the crows first attacked him. In that moment, Crane wasn't a master of fear. He was its victim.

Jonathan stared into Robin's pale white eyes. And then he fainted, falling onto the hardwood floor.

* * *

"Careful men," Commissioner Gordon said to the EMTs as they carried Jonathan Crane on a stretcher toward their parked ambulance. "Let's not lose this one, all right?"

The technicians didn't answer. But they didn't seem too concerned, either. Crane was handcuffed and unconscious. The villain looked about as harmful as a sleeping puppy.

Gordon put his hands in the pockets of his trench coat as the wind picked up. His hair blew in the cold breeze. He walked away from the flashing lights of the police cars and the flash bulbs of the press's cameras. A few moments later, he was standing in the alley beside the hotel.

"I admit it, you had me fooled," Commissioner Gordon said to someone hiding in the shadows.

"Sorry about that," a voice rumbled. Batman stepped out into the moonlight. "We needed Crane to think he'd really killed Robin."

"Not likely," said another voice in the shadows. Commissioner Gordon looked to Batman's side. Robin suddenly popped into view. "The guy never had a chance."

"You could have at least filled me in on the plan," Gordon said.

"He was watching you," said Batman. "We needed every part of the ruse to look authentic. It wouldn't work otherwise."

"Hmph," Gordon grunted. "I still don't see why you kept me in the dark."

"We didn't know what he was planning, but we weren't about to let it happen," said Batman. "Once Robin realized that Scarecrow was following him, it wasn't hard to lead him to where we wanted him to go. To stop his plan before he even got it started."

"Well your little play certainly caused him to slip up," said Gordon. "He got pretty careless there at the end. But I'm guessing that was the whole point, wasn't it?"

Batman looked over to Robin. "It was his idea," Batman said.

"It was a team effort, really," Robin said.

And then the two heroes pulled out their grapnels from their Utility Belts.

BANG! BANG!

Batman and Robin fired them toward the rooftop of a neighboring building.

"Sorry about keeping you in the dark, Jim," Batman said to Commissioner Gordon. "We're just used to staying in the shadows."

FWOOOOOOOOOOOOOOOSH!

Both of the heroes lifted up into the air and into the night. Gordon watched them go until they were swallowed up by the shadows.

He turned around, shook his head, and smirked. *If I didn't know better,* Commissioner Gordon thought, *I could have sworn I just saw Batman crack a smile.*

*   *   *

Jonathan Crane woke up in a pool of his own sweat. His eyes darted around the walls of his small Arkham Asylum cell. He looked from one shadow to another quickly. He desperately wanted to make sure that he was alone.

He just had that dream again. It was the one where he was a little boy running from crows. And then the crows changed to bats. And then the bats got closer. And out from the middle of them . . .

Crane couldn't bear to think of it.

The dream tonight was worse than it had ever been. Because it was no longer a giant bat that he saw when he closed his eyes. It was a different flying creature that now haunted his nightmares.

TAP! TAP! TAP!

Jonathan's eyes went wide. He looked over at the small window of his cell. There was nothing there. But he had heard —

TAP! TAP! TAP!

He buried his head underneath his blanket. The noise was a familiar one. It could only be one thing.

TAP! TAP! TAP! TAP! TAP! TAP!

The noise grew worse. It was deafening. It was the creature from his nightmares.

Crane couldn't escape it. No matter where he went, the ghost of Robin was watching him. Following him.

Haunting him.

TAP! TAP! TAP!

TAP! TAP! TAP!

TAP! TAP! TAP!

Jonathan Crane curled up into a little ball. He closed his eyes as tightly as he could. The tapping continued.

Crane cautiously opened an eye and looked up toward his window.

TAP! TAP! TAP!

A robin was tapping at the bars of his cell.

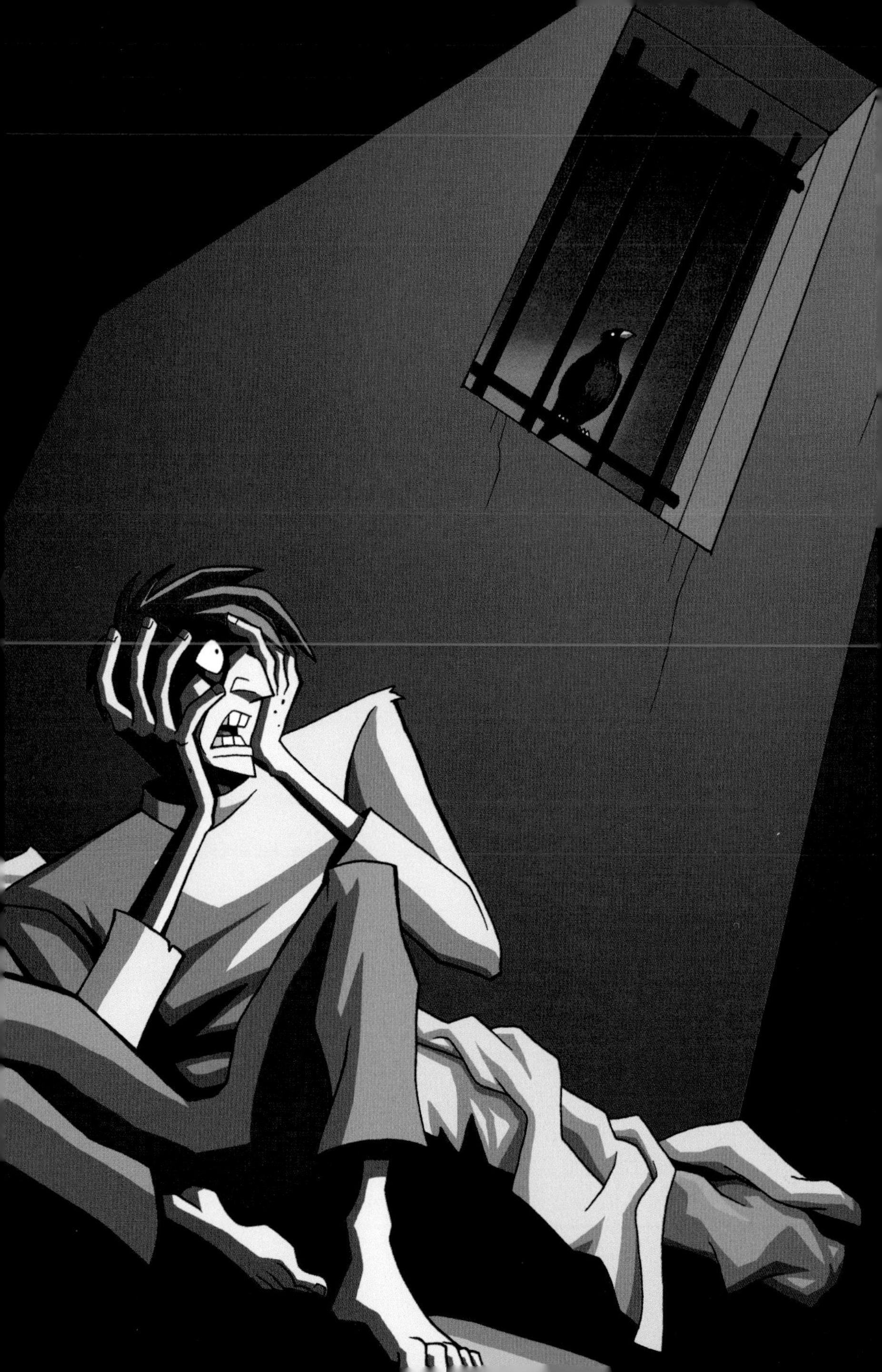

SCARECROW

REAL NAME:
Jonathan Crane

OCCUPATION:
Professional Criminal

BASE:
Gotham City

HEIGHT:
6 feet

WEIGHT:
140 pounds

EYES:
Blue

HAIR:
Brown

Jonathan Crane's obsession with fear took hold at an early age. Terrorized by bullies, Crane sought to free himself of his own worst fears. As he researched the subject of dread, Crane became an expert on fear. Using this knowledge, Crane overcame his tormentors by using their worst fears against them. This victory led to his transformation into the super-villain, the Scarecrow.

- Crane became a professor to further his terrifying research. But when his colleagues took notice of his sick experiments, they had him fired. To get revenge, Crane tried to scare them to death.

- Crane's Fear Toxin brings his victims' worst fears and phobias to life. The gas also makes the frail Crane look like a fearsome predator in the eyes of his prey.

- Even though he preys on the fears of others, the Scarecrow has a fear of his own — bats! Crane has been chiropteraphobic, or afraid of bats, since his first encounter with the Dark Knight.

- Crane's mastery of fear has come in handy. While locked up in Arkham Asylum, Crane escaped from his cell by scaring two guards into releasing him.

BIOGRAPHIES

MATTHEW K. MANNING is the author of many books and comics, from the massive Andrews McMeel hardcover *The Batman Files* to single issues of comic books such as Looney Tunes. He recently penned a mini-series for DC Comics, and is developing another new original series. He lives in Mystic, Connecticut with his wife, Dorothy, and his daughter, Lillian.

LUCIANO VECCHIO was born in 1982 and currently lives in Buenos Aires, Argentina. With experience in illustration, animation, and comics, his works have been published in the US, Spain, UK, France and Argentina. Credits include *Ben 10* (DC Comics), *Cruel Thing* (Norma), *Unseen Tribe* (Zuda Comics), and *Sentinels* (Drumfish Productions).

GLOSSARY

batch (BACH)—a group of things that arrive together or are made together, as in a batch of cookies

cautiously (KAW-shuhss-lee)—very carefully or apprehensively

eerie (EER-ee)—strange and frightening

foul (FOUL)—very dirty or disgusting

overwhelm (oh-vur-WELM)—to have a very strong effect, or to defeat or overcome completely

pace (PAYSS)—a rate of speed

pale (PAYL)—having a light skin color, or not bright in color

perspective (pur-SPEK-tiv)—a particular way of looking at a given situation

phobia (FOH-bee-uh)—an extremely strong or irrational fear

resemblance (ri-ZEM-bluhnz)—if something has a resemblance to something else, they look similar

vivid (VIV-id)—bright and strong, or sharp and clear

DISCUSSION QUESTIONS

1. The Scarecrow is the master of fear. What kinds of things are you afraid of? Talk about your experiences with fear.

2. Who did more to take down the Scarecrow — Batman or Robin? Why?

3. This book has ten illustrations. Which one is your favorite? Why?

WRITING PROMPTS

1. Batman and Robin, also known as the Dynamic Duo, make a great team. Who do you like to team up with? How do the two of you work together? What kinds of things do you do together? Talk about teamwork.

2. Create your own secret super hero identity. What animal is your uniform influenced by? What is your super hero name? Write about your super hero self, then draw a picture of your uniform.

3. Write another chapter to this story where Crane tries to escape from Arkham Asylum, and Batman and Robin try to stop him.

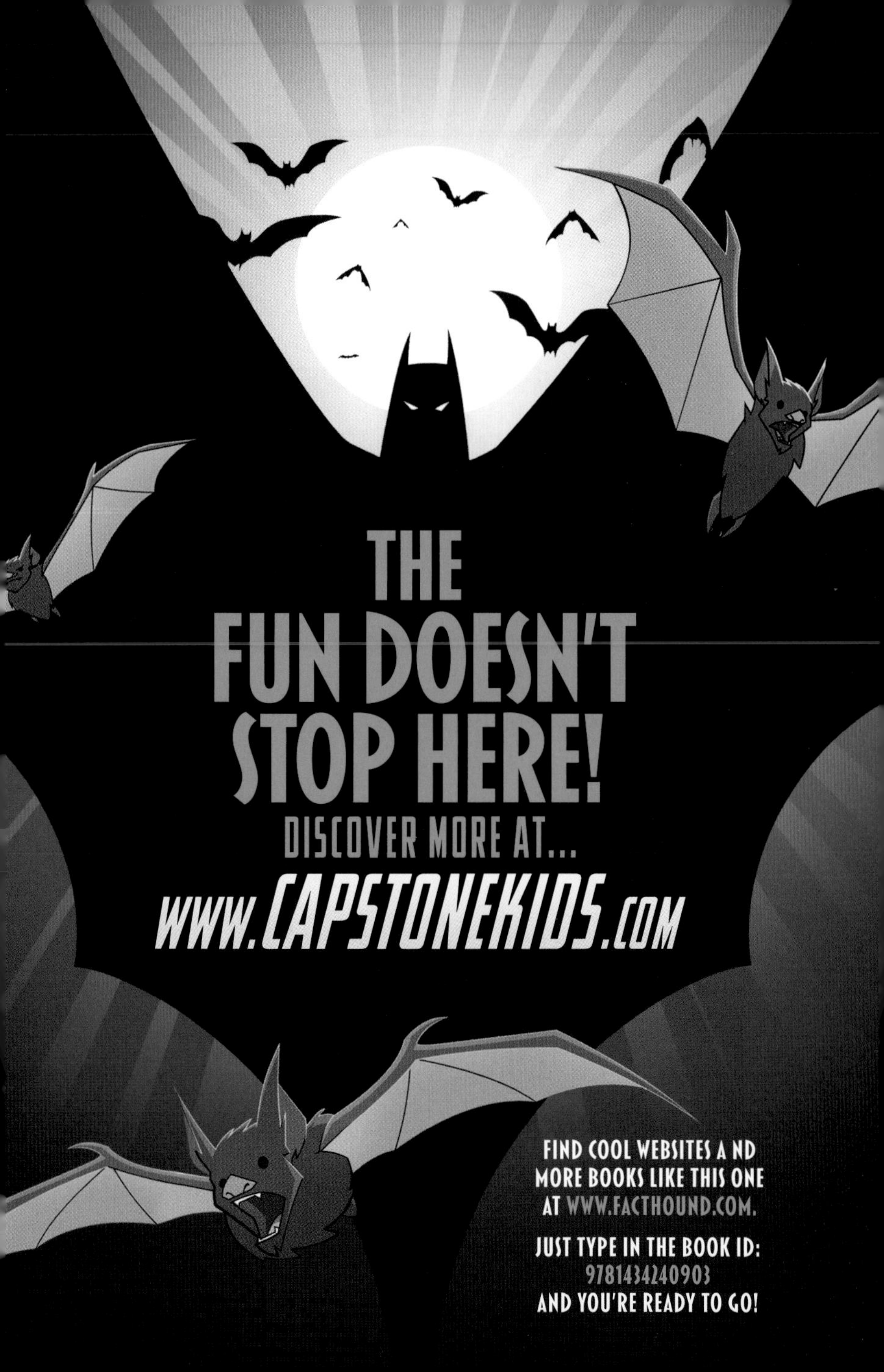
THE
FUN DOESN'T
STOP HERE!
DISCOVER MORE AT...
WWW.CAPSTONEKIDS.COM
FIND COOL WEBSITES AND
MORE BOOKS LIKE THIS ONE
AT WWW.FACTHOUND.COM.
JUST TYPE IN THE BOOK ID:
9781434240903
AND YOU'RE READY TO GO!

LOOK FOR MORE

THE DARK KNIGHT™

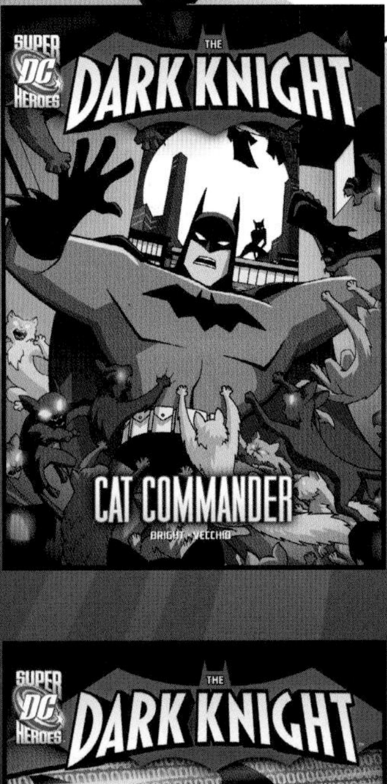
SUPER DC HEROES
THE DARK KNIGHT
CAT COMMANDER
BRIGHT · VECCHIO

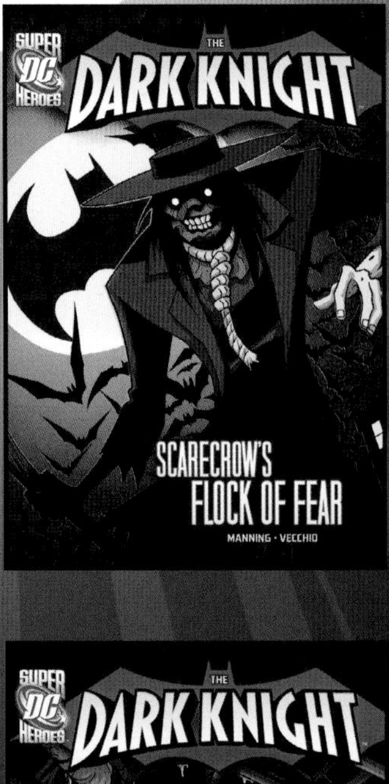
SUPER DC HEROES
THE DARK KNIGHT
SCARECROW'S FLOCK OF FEAR
MANNING · VECCHIO

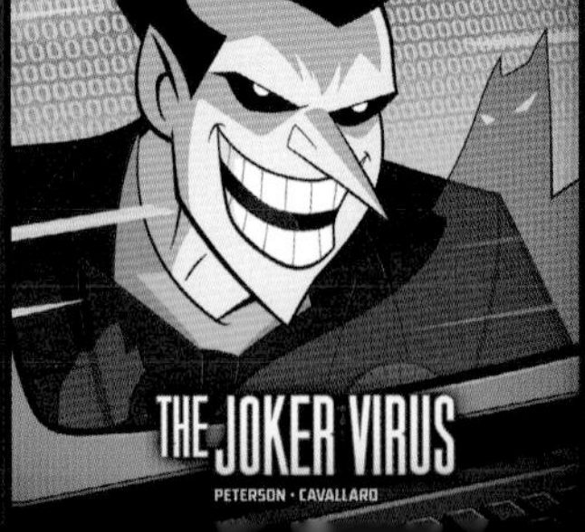
SUPER DC HEROES
THE DARK KNIGHT
THE JOKER VIRUS
PETERSON · CAVALLARO

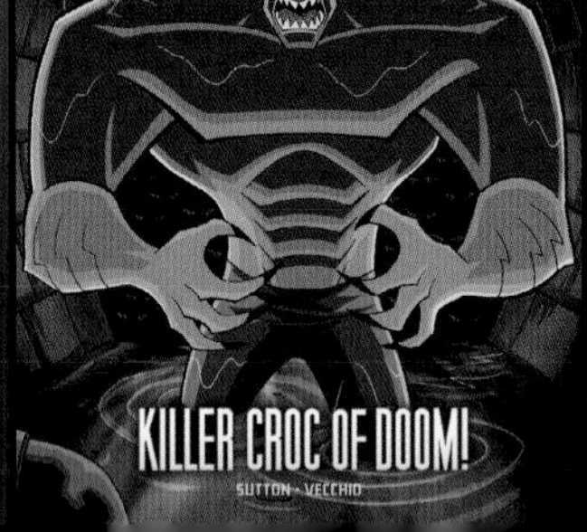
SUPER DC HEROES
THE DARK KNIGHT
KILLER CROC OF DOOM!
SUTTON · VECCHIO

THE DARK KNIGHT™

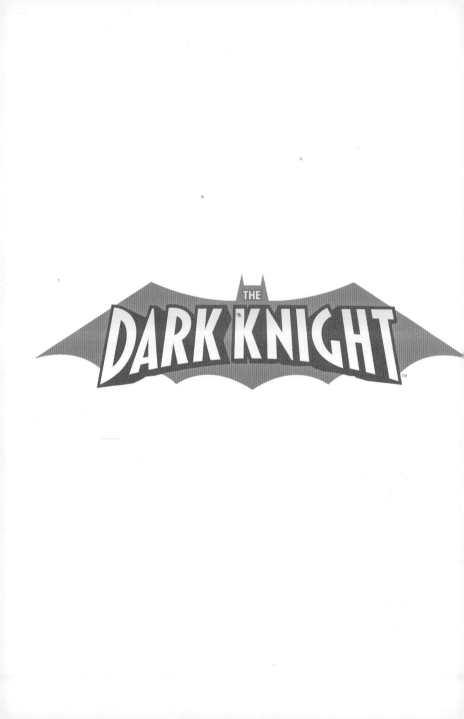